SHREK FOREVER AFTER

WELCOME BACK, OGRE

PSS!
PRICE STERN SLOAN

PRICE STERN SLOAN
Published by the Penguin Group
Penguin Group (USA) Inc., 375 Hudson Street, New York, New York 10014, USA
Penguin Group (Canada), 90 Eglinton Avenue East, Suite 700,
Toronto, Ontario M4P 2Y3, Canada
(a division of Pearson Penguin Canada Inc.)
Penguin Books Ltd., 80 Strand, London WC2R 0RL, England
Penguin Group Ireland, 25 St. Stephen's Green, Dublin 2, Ireland
(a division of Penguin Books Ltd.)
Penguin Group (Australia), 250 Camberwell Road, Camberwell, Victoria 3124, Australia
(a division of Pearson Australia Group Pty. Ltd.)
Penguin Books India Pvt. Ltd., 11 Community Centre, Panchsheel Park,
New Delhi—110 017, India
Penguin Group (NZ), 67 Apollo Drive, Rosedale, North Shore 0632, New Zealand
(a division of Pearson New Zealand Ltd.)
Penguin Books (South Africa) (Pty.) Ltd., 24 Sturdee Avenue,
Rosebank, Johannesburg 2196, South Africa

Penguin Books Ltd., Registered Offices: 80 Strand, London WC2R 0RL, England

Shrek Forever After ™ and © 2010 DreamWorks Animation L.L.C.Shrek is a registered
trademark of DreamWorks Animation L.L.C. All rights reserved. Published by Price Stern Sloan,
a division of Penguin Young Readers Group, 345 Hudson Street, New York, New York 10014.
PSS! is a trademark of Penguin Group (USA) Inc. Printed in the U.S.A.

Library of Congress Control Number: 2009034707.

ISBN 978-0-8431-9949-9   10 9 8 7 6 5 4 3 2 1

WELCOME BACK, OGRE

BY SIERRA HARIMANN AND ILLUSTRATED BY STEVEN E. GORDON

PRICE STERN SLOAN

An Imprint of Penguin Group (USA) Inc.

Once upon a time,

there was a big, green ogre named Shrek.

He had bad breath.

He lived alone in a swamp.

Everyone was scared of him.

But then Shrek met a princess.

Her name was Fiona.

They fell in love and got married.

Once you got to know Shrek,

he wasn't so bad after all.

But he still had bad breath!

Shrek and Fiona had three ogre babies—

Farkle, Fergus, and Felicia.

And they lived happily ever after.

Well, sort of.

Ogre babies were a lot of work!

Shrek loved the ogre baby burps and smells.

But he did not feel like

a scary ogre anymore.

Instead of roaring at villagers,

Shrek changed diapers

and helped Fiona clean the house.

Shrek made a wish that things would

go back to the way they used to be.

Rumpelstiltskin heard Shrek's wish.

Rumpel was a smooth-talking deal maker.

Once, he almost tricked

the king and queen into giving him

the kingdom of Far Far Away.

But then Shrek came along

and ruined his plan.

Rumpel and his goose, Fifi,

had a plan to get back at Shrek.

This was Rumpel's chance to become king.

Rumpel offered Shrek a deal.

Shrek could be a real ogre again for one day.

In exchange, Shrek had to give

Rumpel one day from his past.

Shrek signed the contract.

It worked!

At first, Shrek liked being a scary ogre again.

He chased away the villagers.

He took a mud bath all by himself.

Being an ogre was great!

But when Shrek tried to go home,

his swamp house was gone.

The only thing left was

an empty tree stump.

Where were the babies?

Where was Felicia's favorite toy?

Fiona was gone, too.

Shrek was very upset.

This was not part of the deal!

Some mean witches flew by.

They worked for Rumpel.

In a flash, the witches captured Shrek!

Then they locked him in a carriage

to take him to the new king.

Shrek looked up from his cage.

He couldn't believe his eyes.

Donkey was pulling the carriage!

Donkey was Shrek's best friend.

But Donkey acted like he did not know Shrek.

In Far Far Away, Shrek saw his friend Gingy.

But Gingy did not know Shrek, either.

Gingy was fighting animal crackers

while the villagers watched.

Shrek's friend had become a fierce warrior!

Then Shrek met the king.

It was Rumpel!

Rumpel told Shrek he had

taken away the day that Shrek was born.

Shrek had never existed!

That was why Donkey and Gingy

did not know who Shrek was.

17

Without Shrek around, the king and queen

had made their deal with Rumpel

to give away the kingdom.

Now Rumpel was king.

Shrek was angry.

He wanted his old life back.

He broke free from his chains

and stole one of the witch's brooms.

He scooped Donkey up in his arms

and flew out of the castle.

When they landed in the woods,

Donkey told Shrek not to worry.

He folded up Shrek's contract

to show him the fine print.

True love's kiss would free Shrek!

Then everything would go back to normal.

But Shrek only had twenty-four hours

to get his kiss.

Otherwise his day—

and his life—would be over!

Later, Donkey saw a stack
of yummy waffles.

He couldn't resist.

But it was a trap!

Donkey fell into a deep hole.

Shrek went after his friend.

Shrek and Donkey discovered a camp

filled with ogres!

The ogres were planning to fight Rumpel.

Fiona was their leader!

She was a fierce warrior.

She did not know who Shrek was, either.

Later, Shrek went to find Fiona in her tent.

Puss In Boots was there!

Puss used to wear tall boots.

Now he wore pink bows.

Puss used to be lean and mean.

Now he was fat and fancy.

Shrek was shocked.

Puss had gone soft.

Something had to be done.

Shrek had to get his old life back!

Shrek needed Fiona to kiss him.

But Fiona did not love Shrek.

After all, she thought they had just met!

Luckily, Shrek had a plan.

He gave her a gift basket.

Inside was a heart-shaped box of slugs

and a skunk-scented candle.

It even had a coupon:

Good for one free kiss!

Fiona was not impressed.

Who was this guy, anyway?

That night, Rumpel captured the ogre army.

Fiona and Shrek got away.

Then Fiona went back to save her friends,

but Rumpel caught her.

Still, Rumpel wasn't happy.

He offered a deal for Shrek's capture.

So Shrek turned himself in.

In exchange, Rumpel freed the ogre army.

But since Fiona wasn't *all ogre,*

Rumpel wouldn't release her.

Now Shrek and Fiona were both

trapped in Rumpel's dungeon!

It was up to Donkey and Puss to save the day.

Puss put on his favorite old boots.

Then he, Donkey, and the ogre army

snuck inside the castle and attacked!

Rumpel didn't stand a chance.

They captured Rumpel

and freed Fiona and Shrek.

Shrek's day was almost over.

Shrek was going to be gone forever.

But Fiona realized she loved Shrek.

She kissed him.

True love saved Shrek!

Rumpel's deal was off.

Fiona and Shrek had their old life back.

And they lived happily forever after.